Ralph Vaughan Williams

Romance &
Pastorale

TWO PIECES FOR VIOLIN AND PIANO

ISBN10: 0-571-51432-4
EAN13: 978-0-571-51432-8

Duration: *Romance* c.6 minutes, *Pastorale* c.3 minutes

To buy Faber Music publications or to find out about the full range of titles available
please contact your local retailer or Faber Music sales enquiries:

Faber Music Ltd, Burnt Mill, Elizabeth Way, Harlow CM20 2HX
Tel: +44 (0)1279 82 89 82   Fax: +44 (0)1279 82 89 83
sales@fabermusic.com   fabermusic.com

CURWEN EDITION / FABER MUSIC

ROMANCE
FOR VIOLIN AND PIANO

R. VAUGHAN WILLIAMS

Andantino

PASTORALE

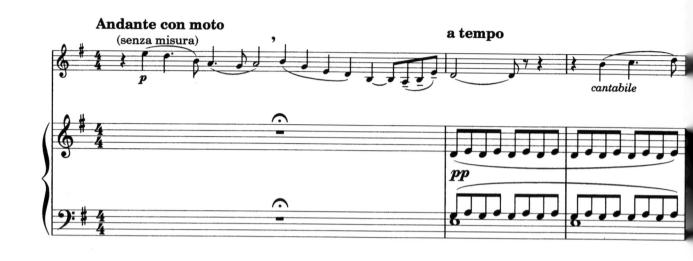

Ralph Vaughan Williams

Romance & Pastorale

TWO PIECES FOR VIOLIN AND PIANO

ISBN10: 0-571-51432-4
EAN13: 978-0-571-51432-8

Duration: *Romance* c.6 minutes, *Pastorale* c.3 minutes

CURWEN EDITION / FABER MUSIC

2

Violin

To D.M.L.

ROMANCE
FOR VIOLIN AND PIANO

R. VAUGHAN WILLIAMS

PASTORALE